AF746341

For Felix, who's had cows.
(In all their *moooooods.*) – KA

Welcome to the world, Olive! – BW

Scholastic Press
An imprint of Scholastic Australia Pty Limited (ABN 11 000 614 577)
PO Box 579 Gosford NSW 2250
www.scholastic.com.au

Part of the Scholastic Group
Sydney • Auckland • New York • Toronto • London • Mexico City
New Delhi • Hong Kong • Buenos Aires • Puerto Rico

Published by Scholastic Australia in 2024.
Text copyright © Kathryn Apel 2024.
Illustrations copyright © Beau Wylie, 2024.

Book Design by Hannah Janzen and Simone Kelleher.

The moral rights of Kathryn Apel and Beau Wylie have been asserted.

All rights reserved. No part of this publication may be reproduced or transmitted in any form or by any means, electronic or mechanical, including photocopying, recording, storage in an information retrieval system, or otherwise, without the prior written permission of the publisher, unless specifically permitted under the Australian Copyright Act 1968 as amended.

NATIONAL LIBRARY OF AUSTRALIA

A catalogue record for this book is available from the National Library of Australia

ISBN: 978-1-76112-765-6

Typeset in Bodoni Hand.

The illustrations in this book were painted digitally.

Printed in China by RR Donnelley.

Scholastic Australia's policy, in association with RR Donnelley, is to use papers that are renewable and made efficiently from wood grown in responsibly managed sources, so as to minimise its environmental footprint.

10 9 8 7 6 5 4 3 2 1 24 25 26 27 28 / 2

KATHRYN APEL & BEAU WYLIE

MAD COWS

A Scholastic Press book from Scholastic Australia

Glad cows.

Sad cows.

Mad cows.

Bad cows.

Add cows.

Glad cows.

Mad cows.

Bad cows.

Sad cows.

Glad cows.

Sad cows.

Mad cows.

Bad cows.

Add cows.

Rad cows.

Glad cows.

Bad cows.

Glad cows.

Nomad cows.

'We *had* cows!'